Bernard Goes to School

BERNARD GOES TO SCHOOL

by Joan Elizabeth Goodman

Illustrated by
Dominic Catalano

Boyds Mills Press

For Pat,
Thanks for the last word
—J. E. G.

For my grandfather, who brought joy to my early years
—D. C.

Text copyright © 2001 by Joan Elizabeth Goodman
Illustrations copyright © 2001 by Dominic Catalano

Published by Caroline House
Boyds Mills Press, Inc.
A Highlights Company
815 Church Street
Honesdale, Pennsylvania 18431
Printed in China

U.S. Cataloging-in-Publication Data
   (Library of Congress Standards)

Goodman, Joan Elizabeth.
    Bernard goes to school / by Joan Elizabeth Goodman ; illustrated
by Dominic Catalano.—1st ed.
[32]p. : col. Ill. ; cm.
Summary: When a young elephant is apprehensive about his
first day of school, his parents show him how much fun school can be.
ISBN 1-56397-958-6
1. Elephants—Fiction. 2. Bedtime—Fiction. I. Catalano, Dominic, ill. II. Title.
  [E] 21 2001 AC CIP
00-103742

First edition, 2001
The text of this book is set in 20-point Galliard.

10 9 8 7 6 5 4 3 2 1

"Here we are, Bernard," said Papa.
"Your very first day of school," said Mama.
She took out her hankie and wiped her eyes.
"How exciting!" said Grandma.
"Time to go home," said Bernard.

"We just got here," said Papa.

"Look at all the children," said Grandma.

"Look at all the toys!" said Papa.

"Here is the teacher," said Mama.

"Good morning, Bernard. I'm Miss Brody."

Bernard hid behind Mama.

"This is your cubby," said Miss Brody. "You can put your backpack here."

"Go home," said Bernard.

"Let's play with the blocks," said Papa. "We can build a castle."

Papa sat down on the block mat and got to work.

"Don't you want to help Papa?" asked Mama.

"No!" said Bernard.

"Ooh! Look at all the hats!" said Grandma, going to the dress-up corner.

"Grandma looks so nice," said Mama. "Would you like to be a firefighter, too?"

"No!" said Bernard.

"I see finger paints," said Mama, "and crayons and markers. Let's make a picture."

"Let's go home," said Bernard.

"Not yet," said Mama, and she scooted over to the art table. Papa was building a tall tower with two boys and a girl. Grandma was having a tea party with the dollies. Mama was already covered with paint. More children and parents were arriving.

Bernard stood in the middle of the busy room, all alone.

"Bernard, would you help me feed the fish?"
asked Miss Brody.

"Maybe," said Bernard.

They went to the fish tank. Bernard counted three speckled fish and one gold one. Miss Brody showed him how to shake the fish-food flakes into the tank. The fish gobbled them up.

"Can I give them some more?" asked Bernard.

"Just a few," said Miss Brody. "Would you like to be the fish feeder this week?"

"Maybe," said Bernard.

A girl came and stood
beside Bernard.

"This is Emily," said
Miss Brody. "Maybe she can
help you name the fish."

Bernard and Emily watched
the fish swim round and
round.

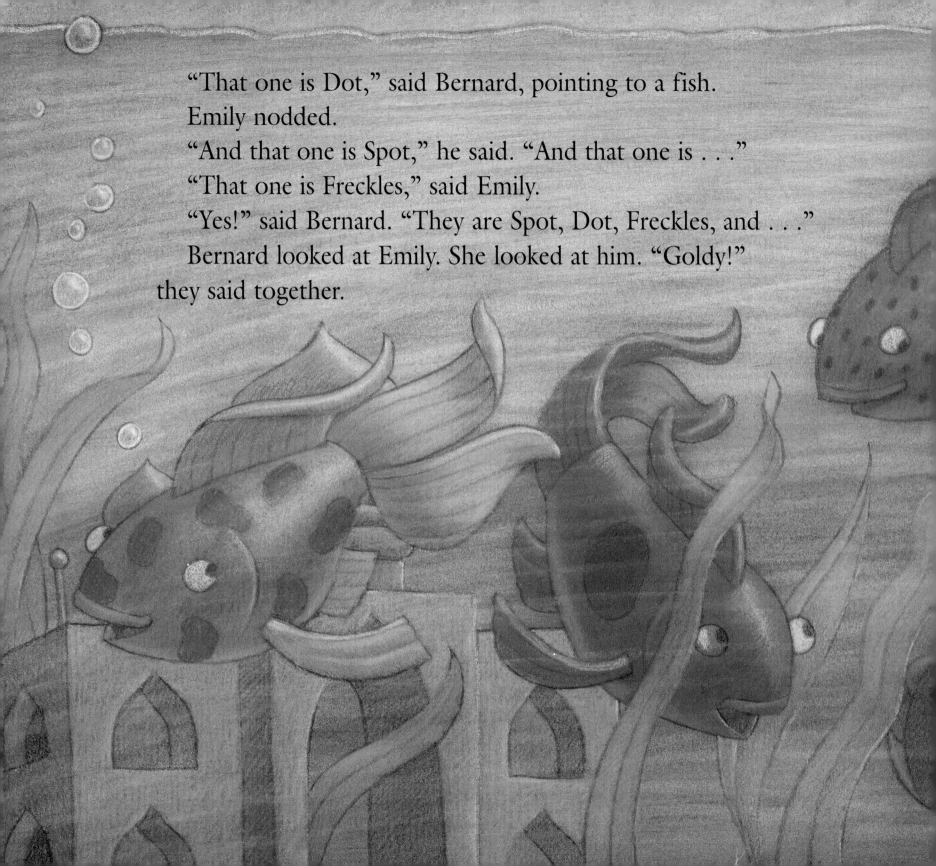

"That one is Dot," said Bernard, pointing to a fish.
Emily nodded.
"And that one is Spot," he said. "And that one is . . ."
"That one is Freckles," said Emily.
"Yes!" said Bernard. "They are Spot, Dot, Freckles, and . . ."
Bernard looked at Emily. She looked at him. "Goldy!"
they said together.

From the block corner came a loud crash.
Papa's castle had tumbled down.

"Oh no!" cried Papa. Blocks were scattered
every which way, all over the floor.

"Too bad," said Mama.

"It was such a fine castle," said Grandma.

"We'll all help clean up," said Miss Brody.

When all the blocks were back on the shelves, Papa said, "Let's build another castle, an even bigger one!"

"Time to go home," said Bernard.

"School hasn't even started," said Grandma.

"You go home," said Bernard.

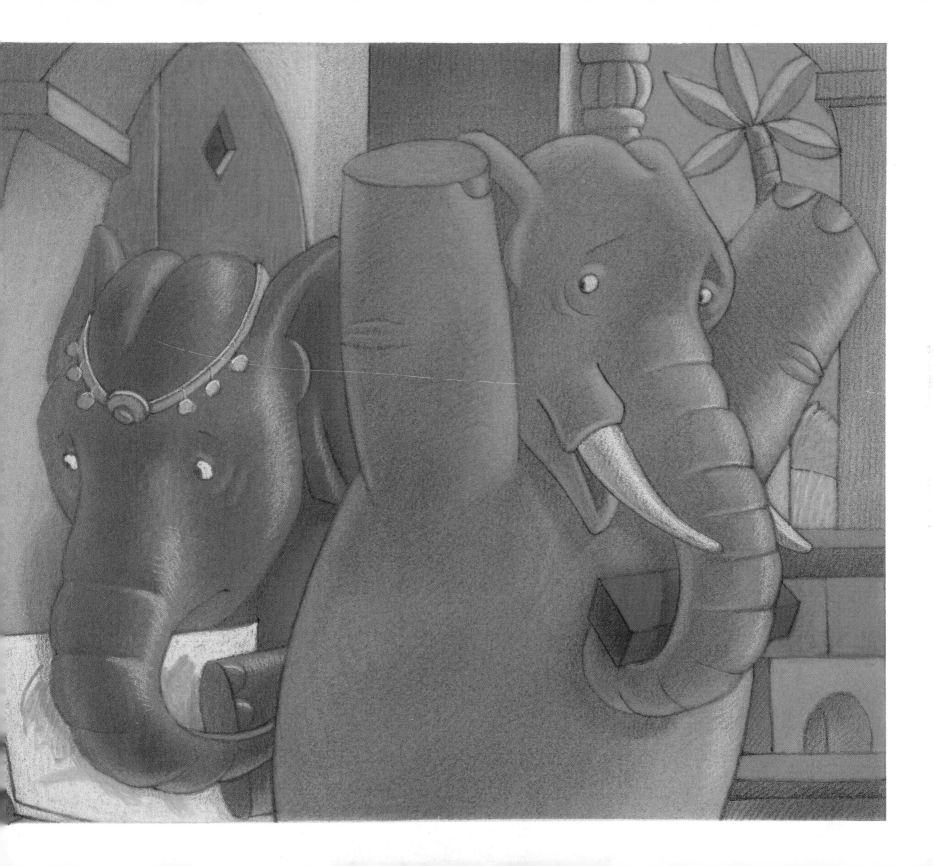

Papa looked around. All the other mothers and fathers had gone.

"Bernard's right," said Mama.

"We should go," said Grandma.

"But we'll come back," said Papa.

"We'll always come back," said Mama.

"I'll be right here," said Bernard. And he kissed them good-bye.